Walt Disney's

MICKEY
and the
BEANSTALK

Adapted from the film *Fun and Fancy Free*

By **TEDDY SLATER**

Illustrated by **PHIL WILSON**

DISNEY
PRESS
NEW YORK

"My Favorite Dream"
Words by William Walsh
Music by Ray Noble
© 1946 Walt Disney Music Co.
Copyright renewed.

Walt Disney's

MICKEY
and the
BEANSTALK

nce upon a time there was a land called Happy Valley. Nestled among the lush growing hills, it was an ever-blooming garden. Juicy red tomatoes, sweet golden corn—the crops ripened faster than the farmers could pick them.

Fat brown cows grazed on the hills, munching the sweet summer grass. A crystal-clear brook bubbled through the fields, and prosperous farms dotted the landscape.

High on a hilltop, overlooking the valley, stood a magnificent castle. It shone like a jewel in the sun.

Within the castle was a treasure trove of precious gems—
rubies and diamonds, sapphires and pearls. But most precious
of all was a golden harp, a singing harp, with the face of an
angel and a voice to match.

Whenever the harp raised her voice in song, bluebirds
chirped merrily, crows cawed happily, and even the farmers
whistled along. The magic of her music cast a spell of peace and
harmony over the land.

But one sad day a mysterious shadow crept across the valley. Darkness descended and lightning flashed. And when the shadow lifted, the golden harp was gone.

Without the magic of the harp, the whole valley slowly dried up. The crystal-clear brook bubbled no more, and the fields of golden corn turned to dust. All that was green turned to brown.

Days passed, then weeks....

The people of Happy Valley weren't happy anymore. They were sad and hungry! And no one was hungrier than the three poor farmers who lived in the very center of the valley—

Farmer Mickey, Farmer Donald, and Farmer Goofy.

These fine friends had always lived and worked together, without a care or a woe. But now their land was barren, and their once-full cupboard was practically bare. All that remained was a stale loaf of bread and a small crock of beans.

Mickey, Donald, and Goofy rationed out their meager meals, washing them down with milk from their cow, Bossy.

Even so, there came a day when nothing was left but one crust of bread and one lone bean. As usual, the friends shared this last pitiful meal. The bread was sliced so thin that Mickey could see right through it to his one-third of a bean! And now there wasn't even anything to drink. Poor Bossy had stopped giving milk, for she was starving, too.

"We have to get more food!" Donald cried.

"But how?" Goofy wailed. "We've got no money. We've got no crops. We've got no nuthin'! What're we gonna do?"

"Don't worry," Mickey said brightly. "We still have one thing left—Bossy! We can sell the cow and buy some food."

"Sell old Bossy?" Donald cried.

"Aw, we couldn't do that," said Goofy. "Bossy isn't just a cow—she's our friend."

Mickey slowly nodded his head in agreement, but he knew there was no other way. He would have to take Bossy to town and sell her.

Goofy bid Bossy a sad good-bye, but after a while his spirits
revived. The mere thought of the food to come brought a smile
to his face.

While they waited, Goofy and Donald imagined the goodies
Mickey would bring. They chanted together, "Lobster, turkey,
sweet potato pie..."

"Pancakes piled up till they reach the sky," Donald added.

"Lots of starches," Goofy chimed, "lots of greens, lots of
chocolate-covered..."

"Beans!" Mickey cried, flinging open the door and proudly
holding out a little green box.

"Beans?" Donald cried in disbelief. "You mean you sold our cow for a bunch of beans?"

"Oh, but these aren't ordinary beans," Mickey assured him, taking three quite ordinary looking beans from the box. "These are magic beans. If we plant them in the light of a full moon, do you know what we'll get?"

"*More beans,*" muttered Donald in disgust. Then he grabbed the beans from Mickey's hand and flung them to the ground.

"Oh no!" Mickey cried, horrified as the beans rolled across the wooden floor and fell through a hole.

That night the farmers went to bed hungrier than ever. They soon fell into a fitful sleep.

While Mickey, Donald, and Goofy tossed and turned, a silvery moonbeam spilled in through the open window and disappeared into the very hole the beans had fallen through.

For a long time all that could be heard was the soft snuffle of Goofy's snores and the rumble-grumble of Donald's empty stomach. But then there came a strange swishing sound as a tender green shoot emerged from the hole.

Slowly the young vine slithered across the floor and up the wall, twisting and turning along the way. Higher and higher it climbed, sprouting dark green leaves and long curly tendrils. It wound around Mickey's bed, brushed Donald's toes, tickled Goofy's nose. Then it burst out the doors and windows and into the starry sky.

All through the night the beanstalk grew, onward and upward, lifting the poor, hungry farmers and their ramshackle farmhouse right up into the clouds.

And all the while, the three slept on.

When Mickey, Donald, and Goofy awoke the next morning,
Happy Valley had disappeared. Instead of their familiar farm-
yard, they found themselves in a strange land miles above the
earth.

Eager to explore, they set off at once, forgetting all about their hunger. Before long, they came to a wide moat surrounding a mammoth castle.

"Look at that castle!" Mickey said.

"Uh, look at that moat," Goofy gulped. "How're we gonna get across it?"

Mickey and Donald spied an enormous pea pod at the edge of the water and quickly hopped aboard. Goofy scrambled in behind them, and then all three began paddling furiously.

Halfway to shore, they suddenly felt a whoosh of wind. They turned their eyes skyward as a dozen giant dragonflies swooped by.

"Bombers!" Donald cried with excitement. And, pointing his finger like a machine gun, he yelled, "Rat-a-tat-tat!"

Suddenly one dragonfly turned around, then dove straight down toward the little boat.

"It's coming right at us!" Mickey cried. "Duck!" And that's exactly what Donald did, while Goofy simply covered his eyes, certain the end was near.

Just then a huge fish leapt out of the water and caught the dragonfly in its jaws. As the fish plunged back into the water, its tail slapped the surface, and a great wave capsized the boat. The other dragonflies flew off, and Mickey, Donald, and Goofy swam to shore.

Bravely the three explorers continued on until they reached the colossal castle. It took all their strength to scale the great stone steps. They stood there for a moment, gazing in wonder at the immense wooden door, little knowing what dangers lurked beyond it.

Mickey took a deep breath and knocked boldly. With his hat in his hand, he waited politely for the door to open. But Mickey's fists were like butterfly wings against the solid door; they made not a whisper of sound. Mickey knocked again... and again.

Finally, the three friends simply squeezed through the crack beneath the door.

Inside, the castle was as silent as a tomb. There was no sign of life anywhere. Mickey, Donald, and Goofy gazed around nervously. They looked to the left. They looked to the right. They looked down and then up…and up…and up! And there, atop a towering table, they spied a feast worthy of a king— a giant king, at that.

"FOOD!" they chorused hungrily.

Spread before them were platters and bowls overflowing with delicious things to eat: There was a stuffed roast turkey the size of their farmhouse; a sea of buttery mashed potatoes; an enormous hunk of Swiss cheese drilled with tunnels and craters; and a huge bowl of peas, each pea as big as a cantaloupe!

The three starving farmers shimmied up a table leg and began nibbling and gobbling, chomping and chewing, munching and crunching till they'd had their fill.

Suddenly a soft voice cried out from nowhere, "Who's there?"

Mickey, Donald, and Goofy looked around the empty room in confusion.

"I'm in here," the voice called, and they followed the sound to a small wooden chest at the other end of the table.

Mickey peeked through the keyhole and gasped at the sight of the golden harp, imprisoned in the little box.

"What are you doing in there?" he asked.

"I was kidnapped by a wicked giant," the harp replied.

"A-a giant?" Mickey stammered.

"An ogre with magic powers," the harp went on. "He can turn himself into anything—man or beast. He brought me here to sing him to sleep."

Just then the castle door burst open. Heavy footsteps thundered down the long, dark corridor, and a terrible roar echoed through the cavernous room:

"FEE-FI-FO-FUM!"

A giant shadow loomed on the wall. Mickey, Goofy, and Donald spun around. And there, taller than ten men, stronger than forty, was the giant!

They ran for cover behind a huge china bowl.

But the giant didn't notice them. He had eyes only for the fabulous feast before him. With a greedy grin, he skipped across the room, his big red balloon of a nose twitching in anticipation.

"Fee-fi-fo-fum. I smell..." The giant's voice trailed off as he made his way around the table.

Sniff, sniff, sniff! He followed his nose to a large blue bowl and picked it up in his plump hands. "Pot roast!" he drooled. "*Chocolate* pot roast! With stispashio…stismashio…with…with green gravy!"

Eagerly the giant circled the table, snatching up a plate here, a bowl there. The three farmers kept one step ahead of him, hiding amid the oversize food and dinnerware.

Suddenly the giant reached out, tore off two slabs of bread, slathered them with mustard, added a huge hunk of cheese, half a cooked turkey, and a dozen white onions. Finally, he shook a dark cloud of pepper over it. He was just about to sink his teeth into the sandwich when it began to wiggle and jiggle.

"*A-CHOO!*" Mickey popped his pepper-covered head out of the sandwich and smiled sheepishly at the giant.

The giant took one look at Mickey and dropped the sandwich.
"Gotcha!" he cried, wrapping his big hand around him.

Mickey thought quickly, and, like a palm reader totally absorbed in his work, stared down at the giant's hand. "Wow!" he said, pretending to study the giant-size lifeline. "It says here that you can change yourself into anything!"

"Yup!" the giant said proudly, setting Mickey down on the table beside a giant flyswatter. "Wanna see? Go on, give me something—anything."

"Anything?" Mickey said slyly, trying not to stare at the fly-swatter—or at his two friends peeking out of the salt and pepper shakers.

After pretending to think a while, Mickey finally said, "I bet you can't change into a teeny-weeny fly."

"I can do better than that," the eager giant boasted. "How about a fluffy pink bunny with long pink ears?"

But Mickey would hear of nothing less—or more!—than a teeny-weeny fly.

"Well, if that's what you really want," the giant said with disappointment. "I'll just say the magic words: *Fee-fi-fo-fum!*" And with that, he began to whirl around, faster and faster, till he was only a blur.

Mickey, Donald, and Goofy picked up the flyswatter and got
ready to pounce just as the giant stopped spinning. But instead
of the teeny-weeny fly they were expecting to see, they found
themselves face-to-face with an enormous pink rabbit.

"You sure you don't want a bunny?" the giant said cheerfully.
But his smile faded and his ears drooped when he caught sight
of the three farmers armed with the flyswatter.

Now the giant was angry. "You think you fool me?" he roared, scooping Mickey, Donald, and Goofy up with one gigantic hand. Then he pulled a shiny brass key out of his pocket, opened the wooden chest, plopped the three frightened farmers in, and plucked the magic harp out.

Somehow, in the midst of all that plopping and plucking, Mickey managed to slip behind the box just as the giant turned the key in the lock! He clung tightly to the back of the chest as the giant picked it up and placed it on the highest shelf.

Without looking back, the giant crossed the room and sank into a comfortable chair.

As Mickey peered down from the ledge, the harp looked up and saw him.

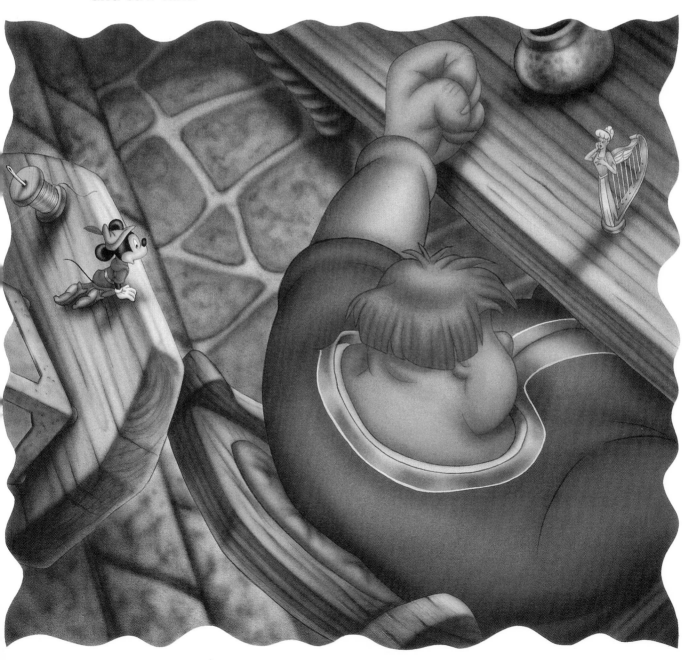

The giant breathed a sigh of contentment as the harp suddenly began to sing a sweet song. Her golden voice filled the room:

In my favorite dream,
everyone is so delightful.
No one's mean or spiteful....

And she kept singing till the giant's head began to loll and his eyelids slowly closed.

Mickey felt his own head begin to bob, and he had to shake himself awake.

Finally, the giant fell fast asleep. Keeping her voice at the same soothing pitch, the harp sang on. But now she was singing for Mickey, not the giant. The tune was the same, but the words were quite different:

> *In his right vest pocket*
> *you'll find the key...*
> *the right vest pocket.*
> *Go carefully!*

Following the harp's musical directions, Mickey carefully
lowered himself by a thread onto the giant's shoulder. Tiptoeing
cautiously, he crossed the giant's vast expanse of neck and
chest before dropping down into the deep, dark pocket. And
there, as promised, he found the brass key.

Unfortunately, that wasn't all he found. In the bottom of the pocket was a tin of snuff. Mickey took a sniff of the snuff and...

"*A-CHOO!*"

The giant's eyes snapped open, and Mickey held his breath. But a moment later, the big eyes closed again.

As soon as the giant was safely snoring, Mickey grabbed the key and began inching his way back up the thread. When he reached the shelf, he quickly unlocked the wooden chest, and Donald and Goofy scrambled out. They dashed across the tabletop, pausing only to pick up the harp.

Mickey lingered a minute longer, taking the time to tie the giant's shoelaces together. He wanted to make absolutely sure the giant wouldn't be able to follow them.

Mickey was just about to tie a knot when the giant's eyes snapped open again. And this time they *stayed* open. With a mighty roar, he lunged after the fleeing farmers. Goofy and Donald made it out the door with the harp, but Mickey tripped over a shovel-size spoon and fell flat on his back.

Before the giant could pounce, Mickey was on his feet again and running toward a gigantic champagne bottle near the edge of the table.

As the giant yelled, "Come back here!" Mickey hopped up on the bottle and popped the cork. And then, as if shot from a cannon, he went sailing through the open window.

Donald and Goofy were halfway down the beanstalk, with Mickey not far behind. Slipping and sliding, he scurried on, with the giant in pursuit.

By the time Mickey reached the bottom, Goofy and Donald were sawing away at the thick green stalk. Back and forth, back and forth they sawed. At last, with a terrible *Rrrip!* the beanstalk was cut clear through.

The three farmers ran for cover. There was a moment of silence and then a thunderous boom as beanstalk—and giant—came tumbling down. Head over heels, the giant fell, over and over, till he crashed to the ground and was still.

With the return of the magic harp, the valley came back to life. The crops bloomed, the livestock flourished, the rolling hills echoed again with laughter and song. And just as they were meant to do, the people of Happy Valley lived happily ever after.

Of course, no one was happier than the three brave farmers who lived in the center of the valley—Farmer Mickey, Farmer Donald, and Farmer Goofy.